THE USBORNE BOOK OF THE SEAS

Jenny Tyler
Assisted by Lisa Watts
Illustrated by Bob Hersey
and designed by Bob Scott

First published in 1976 by Usborne Publishing Ltd,
20 Garrick Street, London WC2E 9BJ, England.

Copyright © 1976 Usborne Publishing Ltd.
All rights reserved. No part of this publication may
be reproduced, stored in a retrieval system, or
transmitted by any means, electronic, mechanical,
photocopying, recording, or otherwise, without the
prior permission of the publisher.

The name Usborne and the device are
Trade Marks of Usborne Publishing Ltd.

Printed in Belgium

Contents

2   The Water in the Sea
4   The Seashore
6   How the Sea Shapes the Land
8   Ports and Harbours
10 Ships in Port
10 Flag Messages
11 Radar and Sonar
12 Lighthouses
14 Currents and Tide
15 Waves and W
16 Icy Seas
17 Islands
18 Fishing
20 Seaweed
21 Pearls
21 Whale
22 Salt a
23 Oil u
24 Expl
26 Div
28 An
30 S
31 S
32

62726   Gr 4up

551.46   Tyler, Jenny
Tyl   The Usborne book of
Copy 7   the seas

Gr 4up

551.46   Tyler, Jenny
Tyl   The Usborne book of
Copy 7   the seas

62726
Siskiyou County
Office of Education Library
609 South Gold Street
Yreka, CA 96097

The Water in the Sea

About seven-tenths of the Earth's surface is covered by sea, yet once there were no seas at all. Scientists think that about 3,500 million years ago the Earth was very hot and surrounded by clouds of steam.

As the Earth cooled, so did the steam around it. You may have noticed how steam on a cold window changes into trickles of water. This is what happened to the steam around the Earth. The water from it made seas in the hollows in the Earth's surface.

1 The sea and the land

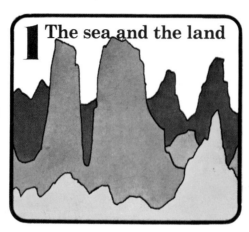

If all the water in the seas could be drained away, the surface of the Earth would look something like this. Some of the mountains would be twice as high as Everest.

2

Imagine all the water being poured back again. It fills the landscape almost to the top. The bits left sticking up out of the water are what we call land.

A water trail

The world's water is always on the move from one place to another. Follow the water trail round this picture to find out how it moves.

3 The air gets colder higher up. The water vapour up here changes into tiny water droplets which hang together as cloud.

1 START HERE.
Tiny specks of water, too small to see, are leaving the sea all the time. They become part of the air and are called *water vapour*.

2 When water changes into water vapour, we say it is *evaporating*. Evaporation happens more quickly when the Sun shines strongly.

Why the seas are salty

Rivers dissolve lots of chemicals out of the rocks and wash them into the sea. One of these chemicals is the salt we eat with our food. When the sea water evaporates, the salt is left behind in the sea. This is why the sea tastes salty.

9 Rivers flow downhill until they reach the sea. Mud, sand and stones that they have carried with them, are dumped on the sea-bed and can sometimes be seen as sandbanks.
GO BACK TO START.

3 This map shows the world's great oceans. The seas and oceans are all joined up and you can travel from one to the other without crossing any land.

4 1,000 METRES ABOVE SEA LEVEL

SEA LEVEL.

Because all the seas are joined the water reaches about the same height up the land all the way round the world. This height is called sea level.

5 1 2 3 4 5 6 7 8 9

Imagine we could rearrange a world map and put all the land together at one end and all the seas at the other. It would look something like this. It shows you how much of the Earth is covered by sea.

4 The wind blows the clouds across the sky.

6 If it is very cold, the cloud droplets freeze and fall as snowflakes.

5 The tiny cloud-water droplets join together— scientists are not sure how—and fall as raindrops.

7 On high mountains, there is snow all year round. Little streams of melted snow run down the mountainside.

8 Other streams are fed by rain water. The streams and small rivers flow into big rivers.

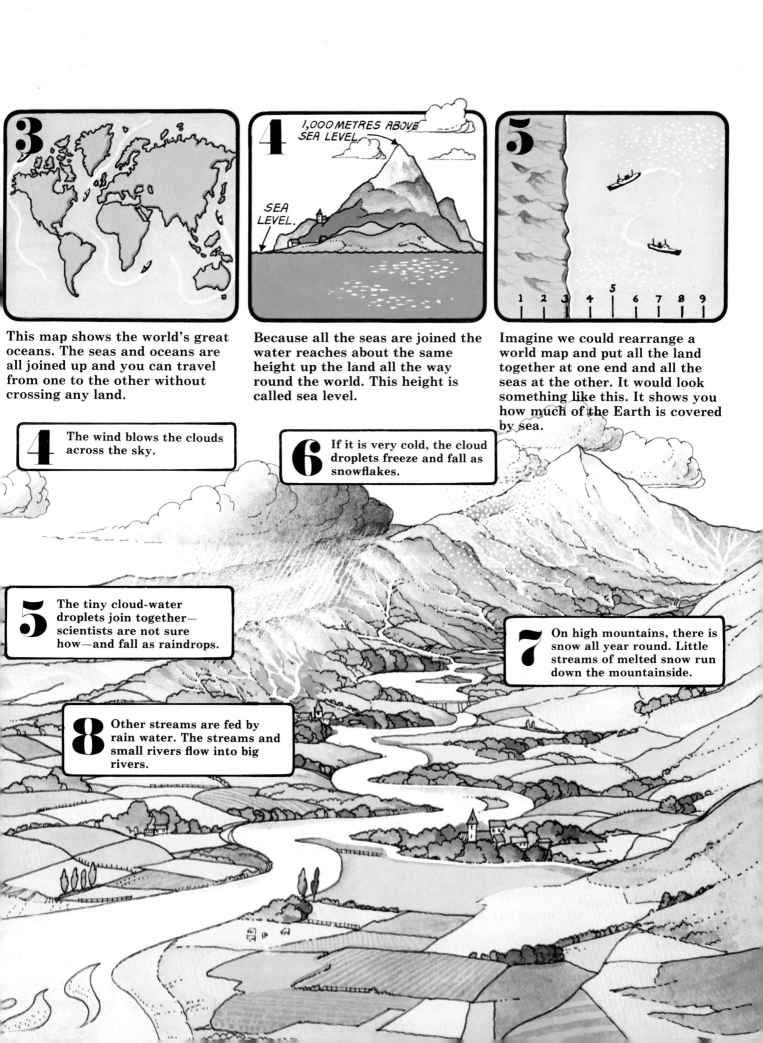

The Seashore

The place where the sea washes the land is called the *shore*. Sometimes the shore is rocky, or it may be a beach made of sand or pebbles.

Near the land the waves in the sea grow taller and then break on the shore in a mass of white foam. The pounding of the waves wears away the rocks and shapes the shoreline.

On most shores there is a *tide*. This is the movement of the sea in and out over the land. At low tide the beach is left bare.

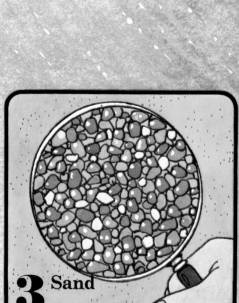

ROCK POOLS ARE TRAPPED HERE WHEN THE TIDE GOES OUT.

BOULDERS

BREAKING WAVES

1 How waves break

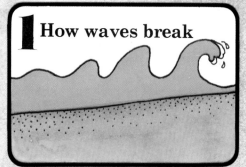

In shallow water the bottom of the wave drags along the ground. The top of the wave moves faster, curls over and breaks off from the bottom of the wave.

2 PLUNGING BREAKER

When the beach is very steep the waves curl right over at the top and then crash down with a lot of noise and spray. These are called plunging breakers.

3 SPILLING BREAKER   GOOD WAVES FOR SURFING.

On flat beaches the waves break more gently. Foam spills down the front of the wave from a little curl at the top.

At the seaside

These pictures show some of the things you might see on the seashore.

1 Boulders

The waves beat against the cliffs and slowly wear away the rocks. At the foot of the cliffs there are big rocks which have broken off the cliffs.

2 Small pebbles

GRIND RUB GRIND

Small stones are carried in the waves. They bang and grind against each other and slowly they become smooth and rounded. Then they are called pebbles.

3 Sand

Sand is lots of tiny bits of very hard rock. Softer rock wears away to become fine mud. Often there are little chips of sea-shell in the sand too.

② SMALL PEBBLES.

③ SANDY BEACH.

LARGER PEBBLES

④

⑤ HIGH-TIDE LINE

SAND DUNES MADE BY WIND.

GRASS STOPS SAND DUNES MOVING FURTHER INLAND.

⑥ GROYNE

SAND AND PEBBLES ARE CARRIED ALONG BEACH BY WAVES. THIS IS CALLED LONGSHORE DRIFT. THEY BUILD UP HERE.

SEA COMES IN FURTHER ON THIS SIDE BECAUSE BEACH IS LOWER.

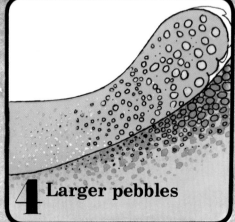

4 Larger pebbles

The pebbles at the top of the beach are larger than those further down. The waves sweep them up there but cannot carry them back again.

5 High-tide line

There is often a line of seaweed, shells and litter along the beach. This has been left stranded by the waves when the tide went out. It is called the high tide line.

6 Groynes

The waves are often blown in at a slant to the shore. Walls, called groynes, are built to stop the sand and pebbles being carried along the shore by these waves.

How the Sea Shapes the Land

Waves are pounding the seashore all the time. They hammer against the cliffs and slowly wear them away. Bits of rock are broken off and then picked up by the next wave and hurled back against the cliff-face.

As the waves crash down on the rocks, air is trapped underneath them. This air is forced into cracks in the rock, splitting them open even more.

In some places the land is being worn away so quickly that walls have to be built to protect it.

1 How land is eaten away

2

3

Sometimes the waves wear away the bottom of cliffs and the top is left hanging. It is never safe to go near the edge of cliffs because the land might crumble away.

As cliffs are worn back, roads and even towns may fall into the sea. About 600 years ago there was a busy town called Dunwich, on the east coast of England.

1 Caves

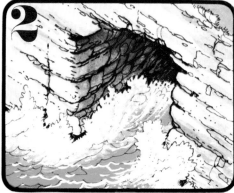

2

3

Cracks in the rock are worn away more quickly than the rest of the cliff. The waves slam into the cracks and slowly widen them and make them into caves.

The waves thunder into the cave and break against the cave walls. Water dashes against the cave roof and sometimes wears a hole right through it.

The hole in the roof of a cave is called a blowhole. As the waves break in the cave below, spray spurts up out of the blowhole.

4

Cliff shapes

Later, the pounding of the waves inside the cave might make the whole roof fall in. Then the cave becomes a narrow inlet in the cliffs.

Rocky headlands are attacked on all sides by the waves. Cracks in the rock are widened as the waves break against the headland. Some of the cracks become caves.

Caves can form on both sides of the headland, back-to-back. The waves break down the back of the caves and make an arch through the headland.

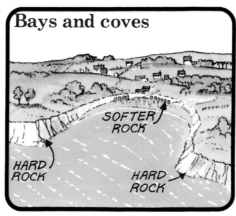

Bays and coves

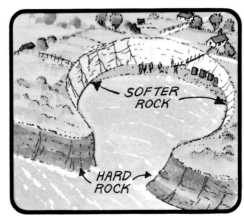

The cliffs slowly crumbled away and whole buildings fell into the sea. Now only the graveyard remains and, with each storm, more graves fall into the sea.

Hard rocks stand up to the waves better than softer rocks. The softer rocks are worn back to make bays while the harder rocks stick out as headlands.

This is a cove. The sea has broken through a ridge of hard rock and is eating away the softer rock behind it. Inside the cove, the sea is calm because it is sheltered.

Land made by the sea

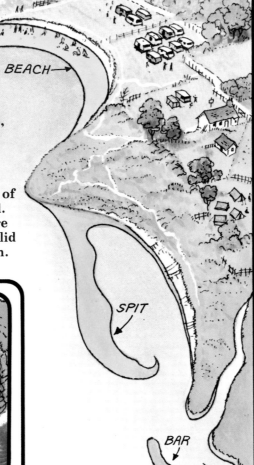

In sheltered places, such as bays, the sea dumps some of the sand and rocks that it has broken off the cliffs. This makes a sandy or pebbly beach in the bay.

Sometimes the sea dumps lots of sand in the shelter of a headland. Sand ridges joined to the land are called spits. Some spits are so solid that people build houses on them.

Rock shapes made by the sea

Hard rocks wear down evenly on all sides. They become very rounded pebbles. You might find pebbles that are almost as round as marbles.

Sometimes there is a crack from top to bottom of the headland. Waves widen the crack until a pillar of rock, called a stack, is left standing alone in the sea.

A river drops lots of sand and mud where it flows into the sea. Banks of sand, called bars, build up in the sea near the mouth of the river.

Flat pebbles come from rocks which are made up of layers. You can sometimes see the layers as bands of different colour in the pebbles.

Ports and Harbours

People need places to keep their ships and boats when they are not at sea. These places must be sheltered from wind and rough seas so that the ships are not damaged and can be loaded and unloaded easily.

Such places are called *harbours*. Some parts of the coast make good natural harbours. Other harbours have to be specially built. Warehouses and factories are built round the harbour and the whole area is called a *port*.

Dredgers

Harbours are sheltered places with calm water, so sand and mud settle on the bottom. To keep the harbour deep, the sand has to be dug up by dredgers.

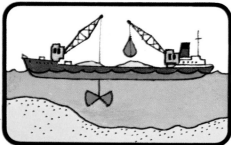

This is a grab dredger. It digs up sand from the harbour bottom and dumps it in a barge. In some harbours, extra-deep channels are made for really big ships.

A bucket dredger has lots of buckets on a belt which goes round and round. Each bucket scoops up sand, and then tips it down a chute into a barge.

1 Why harbours are where they are

A good place for a harbour is in the mouth of a river. Here the water is sheltered by the land. Sometimes the river has to be made deeper for big ships.

2

Another sheltered place is a bay protected by high cliffs. A concrete pier is sometimes built across the entrance to the bay to keep out rough waves.

Look round a harbour

Here are some of the things you might see in a large harbour.

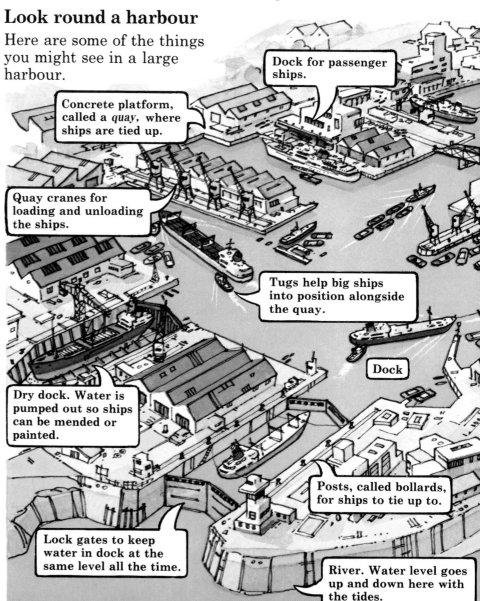

Dock for passenger ships.

Concrete platform, called a *quay*, where ships are tied up.

Quay cranes for loading and unloading the ships.

Tugs help big ships into position alongside the quay.

Dry dock. Water is pumped out so ships can be mended or painted.

Dock

Lock gates to keep water in dock at the same level all the time.

Posts, called bollards, for ships to tie up to.

River. Water level goes up and down here with the tides.

How a lock works

In a small fishing harbour the boats are often left high and dry when the tide goes out. They can leave the harbour only when the tide comes in again.

Big harbours have lock gates to keep the water in when the tide goes out. Without the gates the water would go up and down and make ship-loading difficult.

A *lock* has two sets of gates with a short channel of water between. To enter the harbour the ship goes into the channel and the gates are closed behind it.

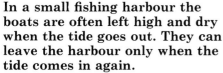

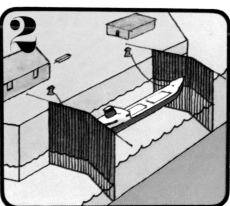

Now the level of the water in the lock has to be made the same as in the harbour. Water is let in to the lock through small gates called sluices.

As the water level in the lock rises, the ship floats up with it. When it is the same height as the harbour water, the gates are opened and the ship moves out.

Ships in Port

Here you can see how different types of ships are dealt with when they come into port.

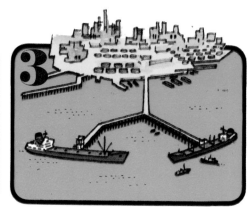

This is a general cargo ship which carries goods of all shapes and sizes. Quayside cranes fitted with hooks or slings are used to load and unload it.

Container ships only carry goods that have been packed into big boxes called containers. Special cranes like this one are used to lift the containers on and off.

When oil tankers dock, they are joined on to pipelines. The oil is then pumped through these pipes to storage tanks on land. The tankers are also filled in this way.

Wheat and sugar are sometimes carried loose in big, bulk-carrier ships. They are poured down chutes into the ship and sucked out again by pipes.

Some ships are built so that vehicles can drive on and off them. They are used for ferrying lorries, trains and cars, and are called roll on/roll off ships, or RO/RO's.

Ships with cranes on deck can unload into barges. These can take the cargo to towns further up river, without unloading it in the harbour first.

Flag Messages

Ships usually have flags flying from their masts. These are not to make the ship look pretty, they are used for sending messages.

Sailors have a code with one flag for each letter. Strings of flags are flown to spell out messages. Most ships have country and company flags too.

Here are some of the flags in the code. One or two flags, flying by themselves, have special meanings.

Letter "A".
Can mean "Be careful, I have a diver down".

Letter "B".
Or, "I am carrying explosives".

Letter "G".
Or, "I need a pilot to help me into harbour".

Letter "P".
Or, "Ship about to sail, everyone must come aboard". This flag is called Blue Peter.

Letter "W".
Or, "I need medical help".

FLAG OF COMPANY WHICH OWNS SHIP.

FLAG OF COUNTRY WHOSE PORT THE SHIP IS IN.

MESSAGE: "I NEED HELP".

MESSAGE: "I AM NOT MOVING".

FLAG OF SHIP'S OWN COUNTRY

10

Radar and  Sonar

1 Radar

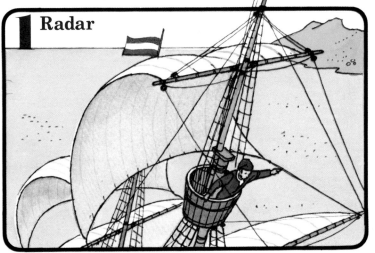

Ships used to have look-outs at the top of the mast to warn the captain of approaching ships or land. This worked well if it was a clear day.

2

RADAR SCANNER SPINNING ROUND.

When it was dark or foggy, look-outs were not much use. Modern ships have *radar* instead. They send out a kind of radio wave in all directions.

3

If the radar waves hit another ship, they bounce back like an echo. We have shown the waves in white so you can see them, but really they are invisible.

4

The radar scanner collects the echo and makes a dot on a special television screen on the ship's bridge.

The ship's navigator works out where the other ship is from the position of the dot on the screen. Then, if necessary, he changes his course to make sure he does not hit it.

5

Radar waves also bounce back from the land and from aeroplanes. Aeroplanes often have radar of their own too.

Sonar

Some ships have equipment called *sonar* which sends out sound waves. These are echoed back by the sea-bed, submarines or even by shoals of fish.

A ship's lights show which way it is pointing at night. It has a green light on its right (*starboard*) side and a red light on its left (*port*) side.

Lighthouses

1 Lighthouses through history

People have used lights to warn ships of dangerous coastlines for centuries. At first, the lights were just bonfires lit on the tops of hills.

2

Towers were built so that the light from the fire could be seen from further away. Some early lighthouses were built of wood, but these often burnt down.

3

Later lighthouses used candles, coal fires and oil lamps for their light. Now most have electric lights and their towers are made of stone or metal.

4

When there is no solid rock to build a lighthouse on, lightships are used. They mark sandbanks and reefs and must be securely anchored to withstand rough seas.

5

Some lightships have been replaced by light towers. The long pole is joined to a platform which stands on the sea-bed. These are safer than lightships.

6

This is a new kind of warning light called a LANBY. Its light and foghorn work automatically, so no-one has to live on it. It is towed into position by tugs.

Buoys

Buoys are coloured metal floats which are anchored to the sea-bed. They warn ships of dangerous rocks, sandbanks or wrecks and mark the safe channels.

Some buoys have rings on top. These are for ships to tie up to, perhaps while waiting to go into harbour. Big mooring buoys are steady enough to stand on.

Inside a lighthouse

Here is a lighthouse built on a rock a little way out to sea. We have taken away part of the wall so that you can see inside. The light warns ships of the dangerous rocks around it. Three lighthouse keepers live here for a month at a time.

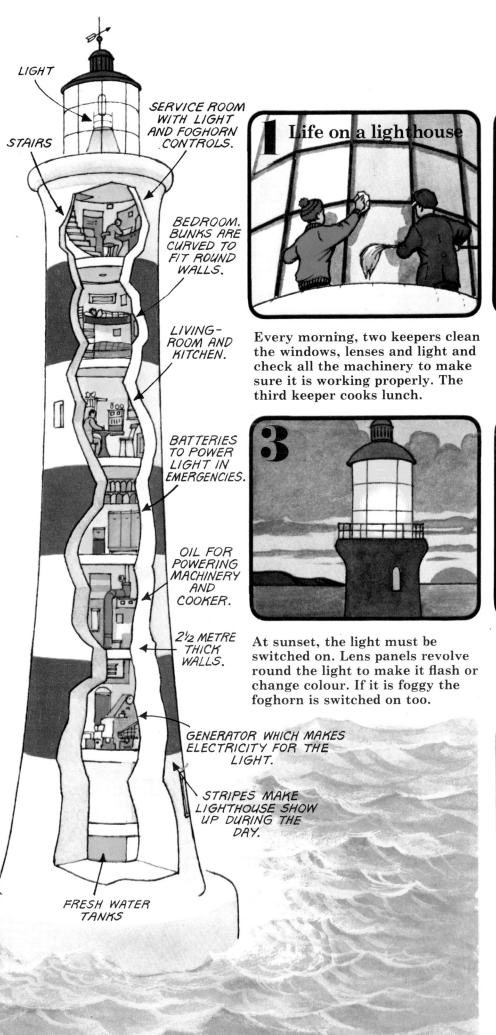

LIGHT

STAIRS

SERVICE ROOM WITH LIGHT AND FOGHORN CONTROLS.

BEDROOM. BUNKS ARE CURVED TO FIT ROUND WALLS.

LIVING-ROOM AND KITCHEN.

BATTERIES TO POWER LIGHT IN EMERGENCIES.

OIL FOR POWERING MACHINERY AND COOKER.

2½ METRE THICK WALLS.

GENERATOR WHICH MAKES ELECTRICITY FOR THE LIGHT.

STRIPES MAKE LIGHTHOUSE SHOW UP DURING THE DAY.

FRESH WATER TANKS

1 Life on a lighthouse

Every morning, two keepers clean the windows, lenses and light and check all the machinery to make sure it is working properly. The third keeper cooks lunch.

In the afternoon, one keeper is on duty in the service room. Another sleeps so that he can do the night duty. The third relaxes and watches television.

3 At sunset, the light must be switched on. Lens panels revolve round the light to make it flash or change colour. If it is foggy the foghorn is switched on too.

4 5

Sailors need to know which lighthouse it is that they can see. Each one has its own sequence of flashes and fog sounds, and these are marked on sailors' charts.

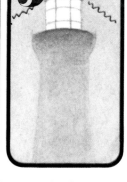

6 Storm waves sometimes break right over a lighthouse and make the whole building shake. The walls are specially built so that they bend but do not crack.

13

Currents and Tides

Currents

Messages in bottles are sometimes found thousands of kilometres from where they were thrown in the sea. How do they travel such a long way?

The water these people are swimming in might once have been at the North Pole. The water in the seas is moving round all the time. These pictures show you how.

Sailing ships used to take a long time to cross the Atlantic Ocean. Around 1780, Benjamin Franklin found that ships taking a certain route took two weeks less.

Franklin made a chart which showed a river of fast-flowing water in the ocean. This is called a *current*. The current Franklin found is called the Gulf Stream.

All the oceans have currents. They happen because warm water moves away from the equator and cooler water from the Poles flows in to take its place.

Scientists throw drift bottles and cards in the sea to find out about currents. Messages inside ask the finder to send them back, saying where they found them.

Tides

In most places, the sea moves regularly in over the shore and then out again. This movement is called the tide.

Scientists are not sure exactly how the tides work. But they do know that the Sun and the Moon have a pulling effect on the seas, and that this makes high and low tide. Most seashores have two high tides and two low tides every day.

This picture shows the tides which happen at the same time in different places on the Earth.

It is high tide here.

One-quarter of the way round, it is low tide.

Three-quarters of the way round, it is low tide.

Half-way round, it is high tide.

14

Waves and Winds

Waves

When you blow across a bowl of water, your breath ruffles the surface into little waves. The same thing happens when the wind blows across the sea.

The stronger the wind, the bigger the waves. The tallest wave ever recorded was seen in 1933 by sailors on a U.S naval ship. They saw a wave 34 metres high in the Pacific Ocean.

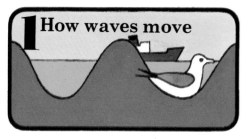

1 How waves move

2

3

Waves travel across the surface of the sea. You might have watched them from the seashore or from a boat. But did you know that the water itself does not travel along? The water just goes up and down as the waves pass through it. When seagulls sit on the sea, they go up and down with the water.

Winds

If you listen to a shipping forecast on the radio, you will hear that numbers are used to describe the strength of the wind.

These numbers are from a scale worked out over a hundred years ago by Admiral Beaufort. It is called the Beaufort scale, after him.

Higher numbers mean a stronger wind and so, bigger waves. Here are some of the numbers in the scale and what they mean.

Wind force 0—no wind at all.

Wind force 4—a fresh breeze.

Wind force 8—a gale is blowing.

Wind force 12 (the highest number in the scale)—means a hurricane.

Icy Seas

If you go far enough north or south, you reach places where it is so cold that the sea freezes over. Sometimes the surface of the sea freezes into a solid sheet of ice. When it melts it breaks into pieces of *pack ice* which float on the sea.

The ice is hard, like rock, and very dangerous for ships because it floats around.

Here are some of the things you might see if you were near the North or South Pole.

Snow is packed down and changed to ice by the weight of more snow falling on top of it.

The ice slowly slides down towards the sea.

Icebergs are carried along by currents in the sea, and blown along by the wind.

Flat-topped icebergs like this one are called tabular icebergs. They are found in the sea near the South Pole.

Icebergs often make creaking noises when they move. Some small bergs are so noisy that they are called growlers.

Icebreaker ships are used to cut a passage through the ice.

Ordinary ships use the passage cut by the icebreaker. Some of them take food and supplies to scientists working near the Poles.

How icebreakers work

Icebreaker ships are specially shaped at the front so that they ride up on to the ice. Then the weight of the ship breaks the ice underneath it.

The Titanic

On a calm night in 1912, a large passenger ship called the Titanic, crashed into an iceberg in the Atlantic. It was the Titanic's first voyage and everyone thought it was unsinkable. But the iceberg tore a 30 metre hole in the side of the ship and within three hours it had sunk. About 1,500 people were drowned.

Islands

When the ice reaches the sea, huge lumps break off and become icebergs floating in the sea.

Only a little bit of an iceberg shows above the water. More than three-quarters of it is under the sea.

Thin, flat pieces of pack ice are formed from frozen sea water.

Useful icebergs

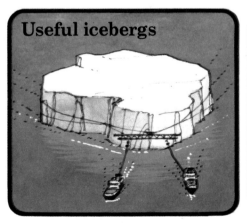

Icebergs are made of snow, so they are not salty. Some scientists think icebergs could be towed to North America and used to water the deserts.

1 Islands are the tops of underwater mountains or volcanoes that stick up above the sea. Only the very tallest mountains make islands.

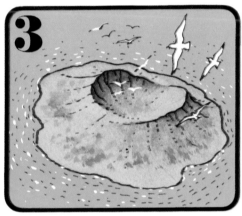

3 The volcano cooled down to form a new island. It was named Surtsey. Now there are plants and animals on the island and people have landed there.

5 Coral polyps attach themselves to rocks and catch food with their tentacles. They grow a chalky skeleton round themselves and this hardens to form the coral.

2 In 1963, a new volcano appeared in the Atlantic Ocean off Iceland. Sea volcanoes often disappear because their ash tops are washed away. But this one is still there.

4 Some islands are made of *coral*. Coral is a hard, rock-like substance which is made by little sea animals called coral polyps. These live only in warm seas.

6 Over thousands of years, the coral builds up to make large reefs and islands. Rings of coral, called *atolls*, sometimes form round sunken volcanoes.

Fishing

This fisherman is on a mosaic that is nearly 2,000 years old. But we know that people were eating sea-food long before that. Sea-shells, fish bones and fish-hooks have been found in ancient rubbish tips that may be 10,000 years old.

Now fish are often caught by trawler boats. These drag enormous nets, called trawls, which scoop up the fish. Some trawlers are equipped with freezers. Some even have factory machines, which can make fish fingers and other fish products while the ship is still at sea.

Here is a fishing port which we have made up to show you how fish are caught and what happens to them afterwards.

How a fishing port works

Type of fishing boat called a stern trawler. Its huge net is longer than a football pitch.

Seabirds often follow fishing boats. They pick up any fish that are thrown overboard.

Fishing boat called a purse seiner. Its net encircles the fish and is drawn together with a rope.

Mending nets.

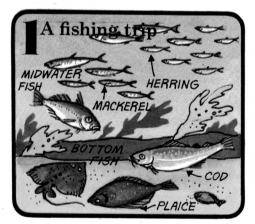

1 A fishing trip

MIDWATER FISH

HERRING

MACKEREL

BOTTOM FISH

COD

PLAICE

Great numbers of these fish are caught every day. Cod and plaice are dragged up from the bottom. Herring, mackerel and tuna are caught near the surface.

2

Mechanical winches haul the full net up the ramp at the back of a stern trawler. On older types of ship the men have to heave the heavy nets in by hand.

3

The fish must be gutted or they will go bad. The crew often have to do this while standing on the wet, slippery deck of the moving ship.

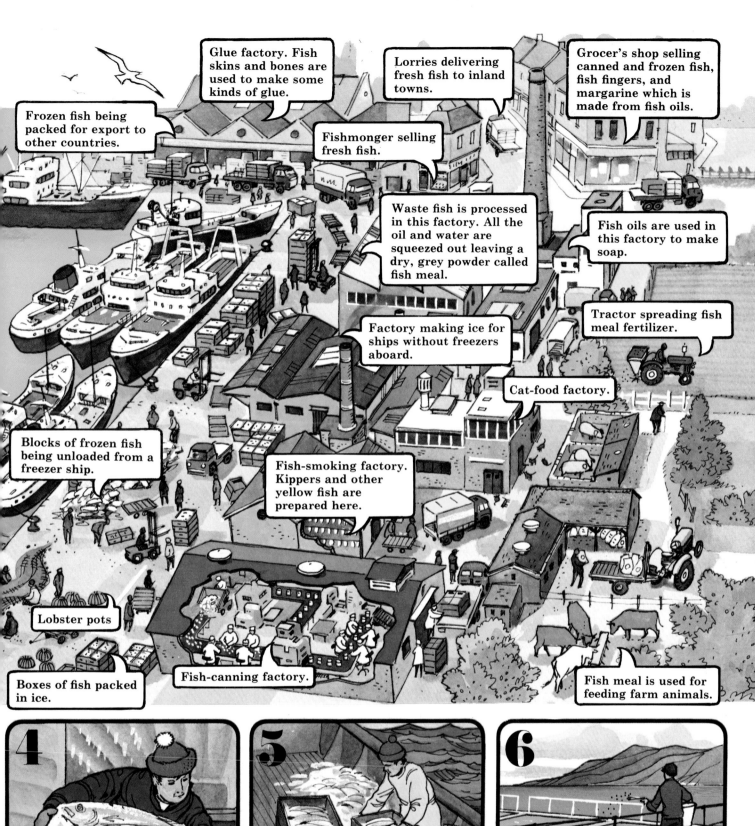

Frozen fish being packed for export to other countries.

Glue factory. Fish skins and bones are used to make some kinds of glue.

Lorries delivering fresh fish to inland towns.

Grocer's shop selling canned and frozen fish, fish fingers, and margarine which is made from fish oils.

Fishmonger selling fresh fish.

Waste fish is processed in this factory. All the oil and water are squeezed out leaving a dry, grey powder called fish meal.

Fish oils are used in this factory to make soap.

Factory making ice for ships without freezers aboard.

Tractor spreading fish meal fertilizer.

Cat-food factory.

Blocks of frozen fish being unloaded from a freezer ship.

Fish-smoking factory. Kippers and other yellow fish are prepared here.

Lobster pots

Fish-canning factory.

Boxes of fish packed in ice.

Fish meal is used for feeding farm animals.

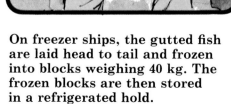

On freezer ships, the gutted fish are laid head to tail and frozen into blocks weighing 40 kg. The frozen blocks are then stored in a refrigerated hold.

Ships without freezers load up with ice before they leave port. Fish are packed in boxes with the ice. These ships must return in two weeks or the fish will go bad.

Scientists are worried that the fish in the sea will soon be used up. They are experimenting with fish farms where fish are hatched from eggs and kept in tanks.

Seaweed and Sponges

We catch and use lots of wild plants and animals from the sea. You will find out about some of them here. If we are not careful, though, we may find that we have caught them all and there are none left.

In some parts of the world there are sea farms where fish and pearls are grown. It may be possible to farm other kinds of sea-life too. Then we could be sure that we were not using it all up.

1 Did you know that ice-cream has seaweed in it? Seaweeds are used to make lots of other things too—like toothpaste, plastics, paint make-up and medicines.

2 The Japanese eat a lot of seaweed, especially a delicate red kind that grows round their shores. It is gathered like this with long hooked poles.

3 An enormous seaweed called giant kelp grows off the west coast of America. It grows extremely quickly and has been known to gain 50 centimetres in one day.

4 Giant kelp is collected by backward-moving seaweed harvester boats. Razor-sharp revolving blades slice the tops off the plants and drag them aboard.

5 The useful part of the seaweed is a gooey jelly which is made by boiling the plants. Whole seaweed is also used for animals' food and for manure.

6 Underwater farm machines may be developed in the future. Then, it might be possible to plant and look after huge fields of seaweed under the sea.

1 Sponges

2

You may have seen expensive, oddly shaped, yellow bath sponges in the shops. These are natural sponges which come from the sea.

Sponges are animals. They "breathe" water containing air and food through little holes, called pores, in their bodies. Only a few kinds are useful as bath sponges.

3 **4**

Divers collect the sponges from the sea-bed. Living sponges are greyish and slimy. They are washed and stamped on or beaten to clean them.

The clean, yellow part of the sponge that we use is its skeleton. The skeletons are trimmed to make nice shapes and sent all over the world.

20

Pearls

1 The shells of some oysters—though not the kind of oyster people eat—contain pearls. This is very rare. Perhaps one oyster in a hundred has one.

2 Oysters are found in warm seas and people dive for them there. Skilled divers, like these Japanese women, stay down for several minutes without breathing.

3 The divers carry stones to make them sink quickly. They fill a bag with oysters and then signal to be pulled up, by tugging a rope tied round their wrists.

4 A pearl is made when a speck of grit gets inside an oyster's shell. The oyster builds up layers of pearly substance round the grit to protect itself.

5 There are pearl farms in Japan. Tiny bits of shell are put inside the oysters, which are then kept in underwater baskets for about three years.

6 The value of a pearl depends on its shape, size and colour. Occasionally, a rare black pearl is found and these are extremely valuable.

Whales

This is a blue whale. Blue whales are the biggest animals that have ever lived. Some weigh several times as much as the heaviest dinosaurs. So many whales have been hunted and killed, that now there are very few left.

Whales have tons of fat, called blubber, round their bodies to keep them warm. Whale oil is made from the blubber. People burned whale oil in lamps before electric lights were invented.

SOME BLUE WHALES WEIGH AS MUCH AS 20 ELEPHANTS.

THE SKIN MAKES A VERY SOFT LEATHER.

BLUBBER LAYER UNDER SKIN CAN BE 60cm THICK.

BLUBBER FROM ONE BLUE WHALE CAN MAKE 120 BARRELS OF OIL.

WHALE MEAT CAN BE EATEN BY PEOPLE AND ANIMALS.

A BIG WHALE MAY BE 30 METRES LONG.

Salt and Metals from the Sea

The salt which we eat with our food was once in the sea. Common salt is a *mineral* and minerals are the chemical materials rocks are made of.

There are about two cupfuls of minerals dissolved in every bucket of sea water. Most of it is common salt, which makes the sea taste salty.

1 Salt

Rain-water and rivers wash minerals out of the rocks and into the sea. Over thousands of years, so many minerals have collected in the sea that is is now very salty.

2

Plants and animals in the sea use some of the minerals. Shellfish take calcium from the water to make their shells and seaweeds store iodine.

3

This is a salt farm which was made in China in 1971. The people are building low walls on the seashore so that they can trap shallow pools of sea water.

4

The sea water evaporates and so the pools dry up. The salt which was in the water is left behind as tiny, white crystals. Then it is collected and cleaned.

Metals in the sea

Mining the minerals from the sea is more difficult than on land. Scientists have invented deep-sea bulldozers and pipes to suck the minerals to the surface.

THERE IS GOLD IN THE WATER, BUT IT COSTS TOO MUCH TO COLLECT IT.

DIAMONDS ARE COLLECTED FROM THE MUD AT THE BOTTOM.

LUMPS OF MANGANESE AND COBALT ARE SUCKED UP FROM THE SEA FLOOR.

Making fresh water

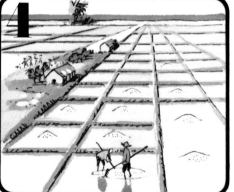

SALTY SEA WATER

FRESH WATER IS PIPED AWAY.

Some hot, dry countries have factories where the salt is taken out of sea water to make fresh water. This is called *desalination*.

When sea water evaporates, tiny droplets of fresh water leave its surface, and the salt stays behind. This fresh water is collected and piped away.

Oil under the Sea

In rocks deep under the sea, there are tiny drops of oil. To reach the oil a hole is drilled from a drilling rig right down into the sea-bed.

Scientists think oil is probably made from the bodies of tiny sea creatures which lived millions of years ago. When the creatures died they were buried by mud and sand, and slowly they changed into little drops of oil.

Over millions of years, thick layers of mud have settled at the bottom of the sea and hardened to form layers of rock on top of the oil.

This is the derrick which supports the drilling pipes.

The crew are brought to the rig by helicopter. Usually they stay on the rig for 14 days and then go ashore for 14 days. About a hundred men live on the rig.

Underwater divers check the anchors and drilling pipes to make sure they are secure. The rig has to be held very firmly in position, especially when the sea is rough.

These workers are called roughnecks. Here they are adding another pipe to the drill so they can bore deeper into the rocks of the sea-bed.

DIAMONDS

The drilling bits have to be very strong to cut through the rocks. They are made of specially strengthened steel and some are studded with diamonds.

Exploring the Sea-bed

When you are standing on the seashore, or sailing in a boat, it is hard to imagine what goes on in the depths below. Until about a hundred years ago, people thought the sea-bed was completely flat and smooth.

Scientists have now discovered deep valleys and towering mountains under the sea. Some parts of the ocean are so deep that Mount Everest, which is 8,848 m high, would fit under the sea without appearing above the surface.

Diving saucers

People who explore under the sea are called *aquanauts*. They travel in vehicles like this diving saucer. It has a mechanical claw to pick up rocks from the sea-bed.

A bottle dropped in the ocean would be broken by the weight of the water before it reached the bottom. Diving saucers are strongly built to bear this weight.

1 Land under the sea

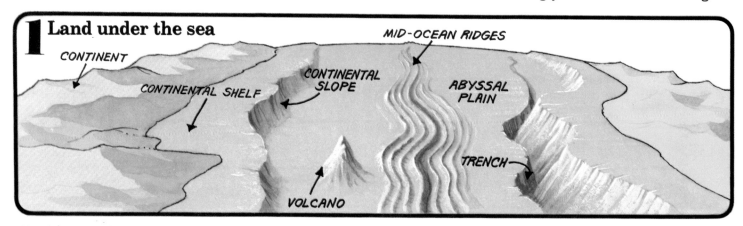

CONTINENT
CONTINENTAL SHELF
CONTINENTAL SLOPE
MID-OCEAN RIDGES
ABYSSAL PLAIN
VOLCANO
TRENCH

The large bits of land which stick up out of the sea are called *continents*. Round the continents the sea-bed is shallow and is called the *continental shelf*.

At the edge of the continental shelf the sea-bed dips down steeply to the *abyssal plain*. There are ridges of high mountains in the middle of the ocean.

In some oceans there are deep valleys called *trenches* in the sea-bed. The deepest place in the ocean is the Mariana trench, 11,033 m down in the Pacific.

2

CONTINENTAL SHELF
CONTINENTAL SLOPE
ABYSSAL PLAIN

3

Near the land, the bottom of the sea is coated with a thick layer of mud called *sediment*. The sediment is carried into the sea by rivers and the wind.

The mud spills over the edge of the continental shelf like a waterfall over a cliff. It carves a valley in the sea-bed and then flows out over the abyssal plain.

In the deep ocean, there is a layer of sediment called *ooze*. This is made of the remains of dead fish and sea plants which fall to the bottom of the sea.

Echo-sounding

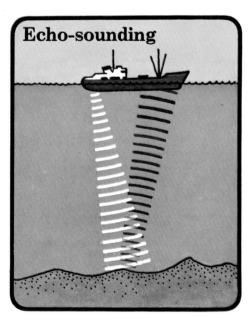

Scientists measure the depth of the ocean by making echos. They time how long a sound takes to echo back from the sea-bed.

Sound moves about 1,500 metres a second through water. So they can work out how deep the water is from how many seconds the echo takes.

Sea-bed rocks

Samples of rock are dug out of the sea-bed with a corer. Scientists study them to learn more about our planet. The corer is a long tube with a 1,000 kg weight on top. It is dropped into the sea and the weight forces the tube into the sea-bed. Then the corer is hauled up with the tube full of rock.

1 The deepest dive

On 23 January, 1960, Jacques Piccard and Don Walsh planned to descend to the deepest part of the deepest ocean in the world.

Their diving craft was called Trieste. In it they hoped to reach the bottom of Mariana Trench, 11,033 m down in the Pacific.

Trieste was a bathyscaph, which is a small, ball-shaped room joined to huge tanks to keep it afloat. The tanks are filled with petrol.

The two men squashed into the tiny room. The walls were made of strong steel to bear the weight of the water deep in the ocean.

When they let out some of the petrol, Trieste began to go down. They sank through the water at a speed of a metre a second.

At 400 metres it grew dark, for hardly any sunlight filters this deep. They switched on the spotlight and saw coloured fish.

After four hours, they reckoned they were near the bottom. To slow down, they made Trieste lighter by throwing out lead weights.

A cloud of mud billowed round them as they landed, and then they saw a fish swimming in the sea at the bottom of the world.

Divers

Until about a hundred years ago, people could stay under water for only as long as they could hold their breath. Then the first diving suits were made. The diver wore a big helmet and air was pumped into the helmet through a pipe. The diver had to be very careful not to get his air pipe twisted.

Now, people can swim under water almost as freely as fish. They carry their own air in a piece of apparatus called an *aqualung*. This was invented about 30 years ago.

1 Aqualunging

An aqualung diver straps cannisters of air on his back and breathes the air through a mouthpiece. There is usually enough air for an hour's swim.

2

There is plenty of work under the sea for aqualung divers. They check underwater oil wells and pipelines, build bridges and study sea life and the sea-bed.

3

Divers use special waterproof cameras to take pictures of sea animals and the land under the sea. They need to use flashlights in the dull, underwater light.

4

Wet suits keep divers warm in the water. The rubber suit traps a film of water next to the skin. The diver's body heats this water which in turn keeps him warm.

5

After diving below 15 metres, divers have to come up very slowly. Otherwise they get agonising pains and jerks called the bends in their knees and elbows.

6

Aqualung divers do not usually go deeper than about 100 metres. Below this, divers wear thick helmets and suits so that they are not crushed by the weight of water.

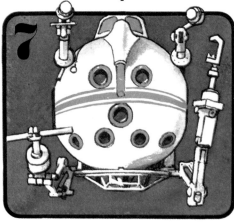

7

This is Beaver IV. It can go much deeper in the sea than a diver. With its movable arms it can work on oil wells and pipelines 600 metres below the surface.

Finding treasure

One day, when he was diving for sponges, a young Greek boy found these statues. They sank with a ship and lay at the bottom of the sea for over 2,000 years.

Living underwater

This is Tektite, a house on the sea-bed where aquanauts lived for several months.

Tektite was anchored to the sea-bed about 15 metres below the surface.

The house was painted white and lots of curious fish swam up to stare at it.

Pipes and cables carried air, fresh water and electricity to the house.

When they swam out from the house they wore wet suits and aqualungs.

If they saw sharks, the aquanauts swam quickly into this cage.

Inside, the aquanauts peeled off their wet suits. They relaxed, played music and cooked their meals.

The aquanauts studied the sea-bed and collected pieces of coral and seaweed or caught lobsters.

Treasure hunters dream of finding chests of gold, silver or jewels in shipwrecks. Now, divers wearing aqualungs can stay underwater long enough to search the wrecks.

Salty sea water eats away wood and metal so the divers have to raise their treasure very gently. One way is to use an air balloon which floats up slowly through the water.

This is the Swedish warship Vasa. It lay on the sea-bed for over 300 years until it was raised and put in a museum. Sea chests, cannons and even a felt hat were found inside.

Animals of the Sea

Imagine you could dive right to the bottom of the ocean. At first you swim through warm, sunlit waters. Then you enter a cold, blue-green coloured place. As you sink lower, it becomes pitch black and the water is freezing cold.

There are no plants down here because plants need sunlight to grow. Deep-sea animals eat each other and dead creatures that drift down from above.

Here is some of the wildlife you might meet on your trip to the bottom of the ocean.

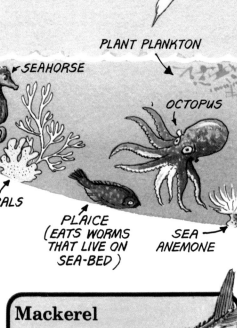

FISH-EATING SEABIRD

PLANT PLANKTON

SEAHORSE

OCTOPUS

SEAWEED (FOUND ONLY NEAR SHORE)

STARFISH

CORALS

PLAICE (EATS WORMS THAT LIVE ON SEA-BED)

SEA ANEMONE

Plant plankton

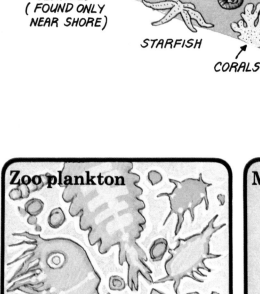

Millions of tiny plants, called *plant plankton*, live near the surface. This is what they look like under a microscope. Really they are smaller than a fullstop.

Zoo plankton

Zoo plankton

Zoo plankton are tiny animals that feed on plant plankton. Some are the babies of larger animals. Most zooplankton are about the size of the letters on this page.

Mackerel

These fish live near the surface and eat zooplankton. They have dark skin on top and silvery skin underneath so that their enemies cannot see them too easily.

Lantern fish

Fish in the dim blue-green waters have very good eyesight. Some have lights on their bodies made by chemicals inside them. These are to confuse their enemies.

Viper fish

Food is scarce in the dark depths. Fish here have huge mouths and expanding stomachs so they can eat anything that comes their way.

Deep-sea angler fish

The deep-sea angler fish has a "fishing rod" with a light to attract fish into its gaping mouth. It is too slow and blind to chase its food.

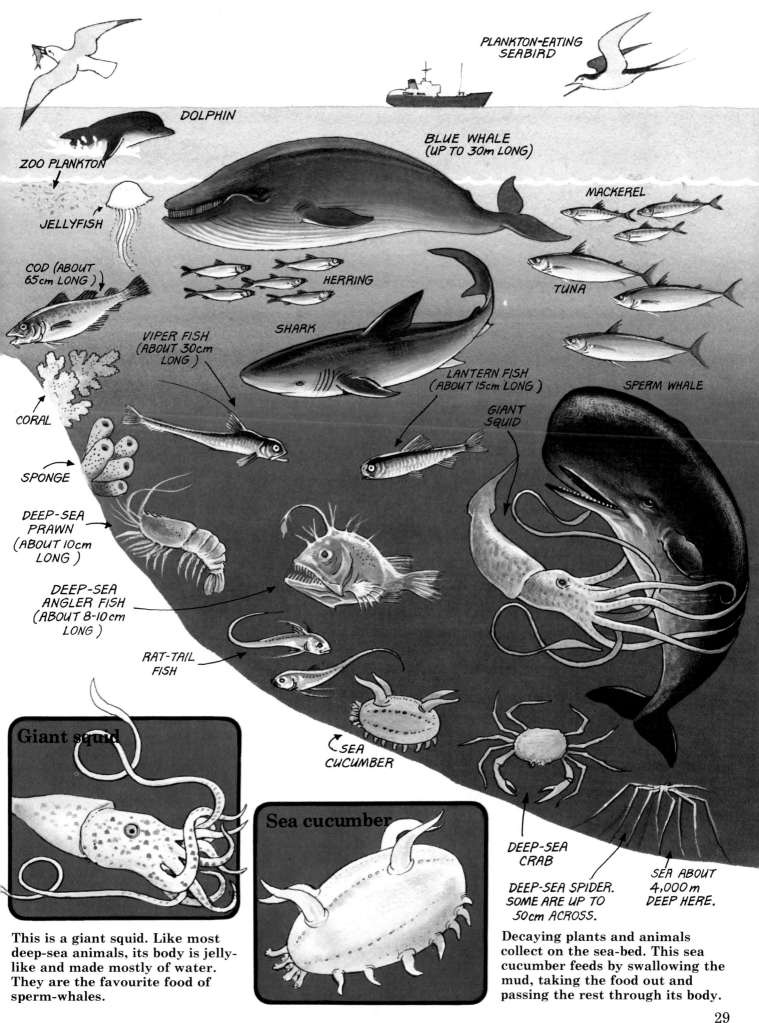

PLANKTON-EATING
SEABIRD

DOLPHIN

BLUE WHALE
(UP TO 30m LONG)

ZOO PLANKTON

MACKEREL

JELLYFISH

HERRING

COD (ABOUT
65cm LONG)

TUNA

SHARK

VIPER FISH
(ABOUT 30cm
LONG)

LANTERN FISH
(ABOUT 15cm LONG)

SPERM WHALE

CORAL

GIANT
SQUID

SPONGE

DEEP-SEA
PRAWN
(ABOUT 10cm
LONG)

DEEP-SEA
ANGLER FISH
(ABOUT 8-10cm
LONG)

RAT-TAIL
FISH

SEA
CUCUMBER

DEEP-SEA
CRAB

DEEP-SEA SPIDER.
SOME ARE UP TO
50cm ACROSS.

SEA ABOUT
4,000 m
DEEP HERE.

Giant squid

This is a giant squid. Like most deep-sea animals, its body is jelly-like and made mostly of water. They are the favourite food of sperm-whales.

Sea cucumber

Decaying plants and animals collect on the sea-bed. This sea cucumber feeds by swallowing the mud, taking the food out and passing the rest through its body.

29

Sea Map

This is a map of the oceans. It shows you the coldest, hottest and saltiest seas in the world. You can also see where some of the things in this book are found.

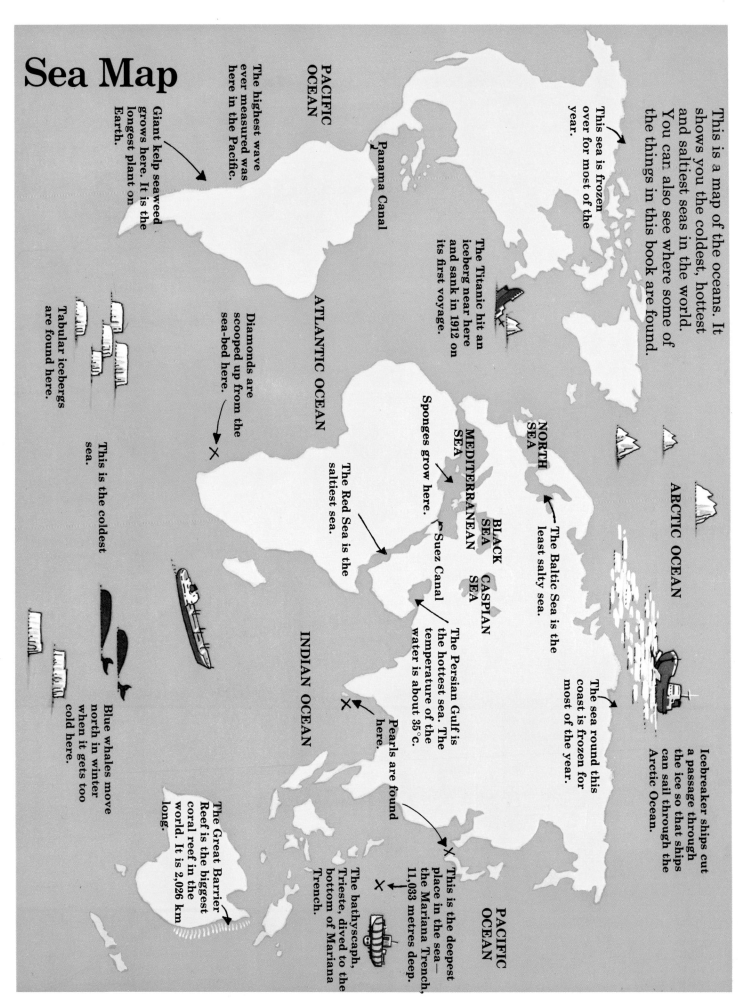

This sea is frozen over for most of the year.

PACIFIC OCEAN

Panama Canal

The highest wave ever measured was here in the Pacific.

Giant kelp seaweed grows here. It is the longest plant on Earth.

The Titanic hit an iceberg near here and sank in 1912 on its first voyage.

ATLANTIC OCEAN

Diamonds are scooped up from the sea-bed here.

Tabular icebergs are found here.

This is the coldest sea.

ARCTIC OCEAN

Icebreaker ships cut a passage through the ice so that ships can sail through the Arctic Ocean.

The sea round this coast is frozen for most of the year.

NORTH SEA

The Baltic Sea is the least salty sea.

Sponges grow here.

MEDITERRANEAN SEA

BLACK SEA

CASPIAN SEA

Suez Canal

The Red Sea is the saltiest sea.

The Persian Gulf is the hottest sea. The temperature of the water is about 35°C.

Pearls are found here.

INDIAN OCEAN

Blue whales move north in winter when it gets too cold here.

The Great Barrier Reef is the biggest coral reef in the world. It is 2,026 km long.

This is the deepest place in the sea— the Mariana Trench, 11,033 metres deep.

The bathyscaph, Trieste, dived to the bottom of Mariana Trench.

PACIFIC OCEAN

Sea Words

Abyssal plain
Vast flat area at the bottom of an ocean.

Aqualung
Cylinders of air used by divers so they can breathe under water.

Aquanaut
Person who explores under the sea.

Atoll
Ring of coral, making an island.

Bathyscaph
Underwater vehicle for deep sea exploration.

Buoys
Floating markers in the sea showing dangerous spots and safe channels.

Continental shelf
The shallow sea-bed round the edge of a large piece of land.

Coral
Rock-like substance made by little sea animals called coral polyps.

Cove
Horse-shoe shaped coastline made where there is soft rock behind a ridge of hard rock.

Current
River of water flowing through the ocean.

Desalination
The process by which fresh water is made from sea water.

Dock
Deep basin in a port in which the water is always kept at the same level.

Evaporation
Water changing into tiny invisible droplets, called water vapour, in the air.

Groyne
Wall to stop sand or pebbles being pushed sideways along a beach.

Iceberg
Huge lump of ice which breaks away from ice-covered land and floats in the sea.

Island
The top of an underwater mountain or volcano which sticks up above the sea.

Lock
A place where boats can be moved from one water level to another.

Longshore drift
The movement of sand or pebbles sideways along a beach by waves.

Ooze
Mud-like substance at the bottom of the sea made of decaying plants and animals.

Pack ice
Pieces of frozen sea water floating on the sea.

Pebble
Small piece of rock made smooth and rounded by constant rubbing against other rocks in the sea.

Plankton
Tiny plants and animals that live near the surface of the sea.

Port
The side of the boat that is to your left when you stand on deck facing the front.

Radar
Radio waves sent out by ships and reflected back to them by land and other ships, to help them see their way.

Sand
Little pieces of sea-shell and very hard rock.

Sea level
The level of the sea, used as a standard for measuring heights and depths of land.

Shore
The place where the sea washes against the land.

Sonar
Sound waves sent down by ships and reflected back by the sea-bed. They show how deep the sea is.

Spit
Sand bank joined on to the land at one end.

Stack
Pillar of rock, separated from a headland when the rock in between wears away.

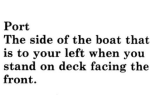
Starboard
The side of a boat that is to your right when you are standing on deck and facing the front.

Tide
Regular movement of the sea up and down the shore.

Trawler
Type of fishing boat which drags a net.

Trench
Very deep part of the ocean.

Wave
Ridge of water in the sea.

Index

Numbers written in italics, like this: *8*, show where a word is explained for the first time.

abyssal plain, *24*, 31
angler fish, 28
aqualung, *26*, 27, 31
aquanaut, *24*–5, 31
arch, *6*
Arctic Ocean, 30
Atlantic Ocean, 14, 17, 30
atoll, *17*, 31

Baltic Sea, 30
bathyscaph, *23*, 30
bay, 6–7
beach, 4, 7
Beaufort scale, 15
Beaver IV, 26
bends, *26*
blowhole, 6
blubber, 21
blue whale, 21, 29, 30
bulk-carrier ship, 10
buoy, *14*, 31

calcium, 22
cave, 6
cliff, 4, 6–7
cloud, 2
cobalt, 22
cod, 18, 29
coldest sea, 30
container ship, 8, 10
continent, *24*
continental shelf, *24*, 31
continental slope, *24*
coral, *17*, 28–9, 30, 31
corer, 25
cove, *7*, 31
current, *14*, 16, 31

deepest sea, 30
desalination, *22*, 31
diamonds, 22, 23, 30
divers, 20, 21, 23, 26–7
diving helmet, 26
diving saucer, 24

diving suit, 26
dock, 8–9, 31
dredger, 8
drift bottle, 14
drilling rig, 23
dry dock, *8*
Dunwich, 6

echo-sounding, *25*
equator, 14
evaporation, *2*, 22, 31
Everest, Mount, 2, 24

fish farm, *18*, 20
fishing port, 18–19
fish meal, 19
flags, 10
foghorn, 13
Franklin, Benjamin, 14

general cargo ship, 10
giant kelp, 20, 30
giant squid, 29
gold, 22
Great Barrier Reef, 30
groyne, *5*, 31
Gulf Stream, 14

harbour, 8
headland, 7
herring, 18, 29
high tide line, *5*
hottest sea, 30

iceberg, 16–17, 30, 31
icebreaker ship, *16*, 30
Iceland, 17
Indian Ocean, 30
iodine, 22
island, *17*, 31

kippers, 19

LANBY, *12*
lantern fish, 28
lighthouse, 12–13
lightship, 12
lobster pot, 19
lock, 8–9, 31
longshore drift, *5*, 31

mackerel, 18, 28, 29

manganese, 22
Mariana Trench, 25, 30
Mediterranean Sea, 30
mid-ocean ridges, 24
mineral, *22*
mining, 22
Moon, 14

oil, 23
oil tanker, 9, 10
ooze, *24*, 31
oyster, 21

Pacific Ocean, 15, 23, 30
pack ice, *16*, 31
pearls, *21*, 30
pebbles, 4–5, 7, 31
Persian Gulf, 30
plaice, 18, 28
plankton, *28*, 31
plunging breakers, 4
Poles, 14, 16
port, *11*, 31
port (harbour), *8*, 10
purse seiner trawler, 18

quay, 8

radar, *11*, 31
rain, 3
Red Sea, 30
reef, 12, 17, 30
river, 3, 22, 24
rock, 25
roll on/roll off ships, 10

salt, 2, 22
salt farm, 22
saltiest sea, 30
sand, *4*, 31
sandbank, 3, 12
sand bar, 7
sand dune, *5*
sea anemone, 28
sea-bed, 24–5, 26–7, 28–9
sea-cucumber, 29
sea level, *3*, 31
seaweed, 20, 22, 28, 30
sediment, *24*
shark 27, 29

ship's lights, 11
shipwreck, 26
shore, *4*, 31
snow, 3, 16
sonar, *11*, 31
spilling breakers, 4
spit, *7*, 31
sponges, 20, 26, 29, 30
stack, *7*, 31
starboard, *11*, 31
stern trawler, 18
Sun, 2, 14
Surtsey, 17
swing-bridge, 9

tallest wave, 15, 30
Tektite, 27
tide, *4*, 9, 14, 31
Titanic, 16, 30
trawler boats, *18*, 31
treasure, 26–7
trench, *24*, 25, 31
Trieste, 25, 30
tug, 8
tuna, 18, 29

Vasa, 27
volcano, 17, 24
viper fish, 28, 29

water vapour, *2*
waves, 4–7, *15*, 31
wet suit, *26*, 27
whale, 21, 29, 30
wind, 2, 15, 16, 24
wind force, 15